Youth

by Thornton Wilder

This play became available through the research and editing of F.J. O'Neil, of manuscripts in the Thornton Wilder Collection at Yale University.

A SAMUEL FRENCH ACTING EDITION

SAMUELFRENCH.COM
SAMUELFRENCH-LONDON.CO.UK

FOR PRODUCTION ENQUIRIES

UNITED STATES AND CANADA

Info@SamuelFrench.com

1-866-598-8449

AMATEUR RIGHTS IN THE
UNITED KINGDOM

Plays@SamuelFrench-London.co.uk

020-7255-4302

Each title is subject to availability from Samuel French, depending upon country of performance. Please be aware that *YOUTH* may not be licensed by Samuel French in your territory. Producers should contact the nearest Samuel French office or licensing partner to verify availability.

For all enquiries regarding Professional productions in the United Kingdom; Professional and Amateur productions throughout the rest of Europe; and motion picture, television, and other media rights, please contact Alan Brodie Representation (Victoria@AlanBrodie.com). Visit www.thorntonwilder.com/contact for details.

No one shall make any changes in this title for the purpose of production. No part of this book may be reproduced, stored in a retrieval system, or transmitted in any form, by any means, now known or yet to be invented, including mechanical, electronic, photocopying, recording, videotaping, or otherwise, without the prior written permission of the publisher. No one shall upload this title, or part of this title, to any social media websites.

MUSIC USE NOTE

Licensees are solely responsible for obtaining formal written permission from copyright owners to use copyrighted music in the performance of this play and are strongly cautioned to do so. If no such permission is obtained by the licensee, then the licensee must use only original music that the licensee owns and controls. Licensees are solely responsible and liable for all music clearances and shall indemnify the copyright owners of the play and their licensing agent, Samuel French, against any costs, expenses, losses and liabilities arising from the use of music by licensees. Please contact the appropriate music licensing authority in your territory for the rights to any incidental music.

IMPORTANT BILLING AND CREDIT REQUIREMENTS

All producers of *YOUTH* must give credit to the author of the play in all programs distributed in connection with performances of the play, and in all instances in which the title of the play appears for the purposes of advertising, publicizing or otherwise exploiting the play and/or a production. The name of the author must appear on a separate line on which no other name appears, immediately following the title and must appear in size of type not less than fifty percent of the size of the title type.

FOREWORD TO *YOUTH*

The Third Play in Thornton Wilder's *Ages of Man* One-Act Play Cycle

From the time he began dreaming up plays as a boy Thornton Wilder's vision of the theater transcended conventional boundaries, and to the end of his life his vision continually evolved and expanded. In 1956, he began work on what grew into an extravagantly ambitious project: two cycles of seven one-act plays based on the Deadly Sins and the Ages of Man. *Youth* is the third play in Wilder's series on the Ages of Man.

In what would prove to be his final dramatic works, Wilder sought not only to explore the theatrical possibilities inherent in the Sins and Ages, but (as he phrased it in his private journal on Christmas Day 1960) to "offer each play in the series as representing, also, a different mode of playwriting: Grand Guignol, Chekhov, Noh play, etc., etc." In short, he envisioned nothing less than a tour de force of dramatic theme and form encapsulated in the economy and intensity of the one-act play.

Wilder did not complete the challenge he set for himself, but he came close. The surviving work enriches his dramatic legacy and deserves to be remembered as more than a footnote to his lifelong conviction (written soon after *Our Town* opened on Broadway in 1938): "The theater offers to imaginative narration its highest possibilities."

The Sins and Ages Then and Now

A brief overview of the history of these plays will help readers place them in Wilder's career as a dramatist. Two Sins, *Bernice* (Pride) and *The Wreck on the 5:25* (Sloth), premiered in English at a special event in Berlin in 1957 (with Wilder performing in *Bernice*). For reasons that have never been clear, for he enjoyed the experience and felt that plays did well, he withdrew them. That same year a third Sin, *The Drunken Sisters* (Gluttony), written as the satyr play for Wilder's full length drama, *The Alcestiad,* proved successful in its premiere on the stage of Zürich's fabled Schauspielhaus.

Five years passed before the continuation of his ambitious scheme appeared on a stage in the United States. In January 1962, two new Ages, *Infancy* and *Childhood,* and a new Sin, *Someone From Assisi* (Lust), opened at Circle in the Square, then located off-Broadway on Bleecker Street, to the reported largest pre-opening advanced sale in that stage's then 11-year history. Billed as "Plays for Bleecker Street," the show of ran for 349 performances.

Then silence. After "Plays for Bleecker Street" closed, no more Sins or Ages appeared. When Thornton Wilder died in 1975 the public record of his 14-play scheme contained only four plays – two Ages (*Infancy* and *Childhood*) and two Sins (Lust and Gluttony).

Today, eleven of Wilder's Sins and Ages are available for production: a completed cycle of the seven Deadly Sins and four of seven Ages of Man. The source of the seven "new" plays is no secret. The missing pieces were found in Thornton Wilder's archives at Yale[1]. From this source, starting in 1995, his literary executor and family released the two plays withdrawn in 1957, *Cement Hands* (Avarice), and four additional titles (*Youth, The Rivers Under the Earth* [Middle Age][2], *A Ringing of Doorbells* [Envy] and *In Shakespeare and the Bible* [Wrath]) recovered and completed by the actor, director and friend of Wilder's, F.J. O'Neil. (Mr. O'Neil's valuable notes on the origin of each of these missing links follow the text of each play.)

The public reception of Thornton Wilder's long lost and new plays was gratifying. *The Wreck on the 5:25* was selected as one of the Best American Short Plays of 1994-95. In 1997, the Centenary of the playwright's birth, Kevin Kline starred in a premiere reading in New York of *Cement Hands,* and the works recovered by Mr. O'Neil served as the centerpieces of Actors Theatre of Louisville's 13th Annual Brown-Forman Classics in Context Festival.   Finally, as the capstone to the Centenary celebration, TCG Press in 1997 published the 11 Sins and Ages in Volume I of *The Collected Short Plays of Thornton Wilder.*

---

[1] No additional one-acts remain to be discovered in Thornton Wilder's archives at Yale.

[2] We believe Wilder intended *The Rivers Under the Earth* to represent Middle Age.

Wilder never followed conventional theatrical practice. As a young writer in his "Classic One Act Plays" of 1931, he swept away scenery and played provocative games with time and place. In the Sins and Ages, his farewell as a playwright, he is no less adventurous by way of settings, techniques, stage-craft and themes. One artistic trend of the day especially "fired his imagination" where these plays are concerned: his passionate belief in the value of the arena stage. "The boxed set play," he wrote in 1961, "encourages the anecdote…The unencumbered stage encourages the truth in everyone." Wilder felt so strongly that audiences should be seated as close to the actors as possible that Samuel French, for several years, was only permitted to license these plays to companies agreeing to perform them on a three-sided thrust or arena stage.

***

As part of its celebration of Wilder's one-act plays, Samuel French and the Wilder family take great pleasure in issuing new acting editions for the Sins and Ages long in print and, for the first time, acting editions of the seven new Wilder works. We invite those performing or teaching these plays to visit www.thorntonwilder.com for additional information.

– Tappan Wilder,
Literary Executor for Thornton Wilder

CHARACTERS

LEMUEL GULLIVER – a shipwrecked sea captain, forty-six
MISTRESS BELINDA JENKINS – a commoner, eighteen
LADY SIBYL PONSONBY – a noble lady, twenty-four
THE DUKE OF CORNWALL – the island's governor, twenty-eight
SIMPSON – a commoner and builder, twenty
TWO BOY GUARDS – fifteen

SETTING

A tropical island.

(At the back, an opening through a thicket leads to the principal town. Forward on the stage is a palm-thatched summer house without walls. Under its roof is a rustic table and bench; on the table some worn books. On the floor at one side of the stage is a piece of glass, fringed with moss; this represents a spring.)

(GULLIVER, forty-six, drags himself on in the last stages of hunger and exhaustion. He sees the spring and avidly laps at it with hand and tongue. Somewhat refreshed, he lies down and closes his eyes. Then rising to a sitting position, he becomes aware of the summer house. He goes to it and opens one of the books. In great amazement he murmurs: "English! In English!")

(In the distance a young woman's voice is heard lilting a kind of yodel. It ceases and is resumed several times.)

(GULLIVER makes a shell of his hands and call:)

GULLIVER. Anyone?…Is anyone there?

BELINDA'S VOICE. What?…Wha…a…t?

GULLIVER. Is anyone there?

VOICE. *(nearer)* 'Oo are *you?*

GULLIVER. *(still calling)* I am an Englishman, madam, ship-wrecked on this island.

VOICE. 'Oo?…'Ooh?

GULLIVER. I am Captain Gulliver, at your service, madam.

VOICE. 'Ooh?

GULLIVER. Captain Gulliver – Lemuel Gulliver of the fourmaster *Arcturus,* Port of London, at your service, madam.

VOICE. Oh! Lord. 'Ow old are you? *(GULLIVER, nonplussed, does not answer.)* 'Ow *old* are you?

GULLIVER. I'm forty-six years of age.

VOICE. *(just offstage)* No!! No!! *Forty*-six! 'Ow did you get here?

GULLIVER. I was shipwrecked, madam. I have been in the sea for three days, pushing a spar. I am sorely in need of food and am much dependent on your kindness.

(*Enter* **MISTRESS BELINDA JENKINS,** *eighteen. She gazes at* **GULLIVER** *with growing abhorrence, covers her face with her hands and turns to the entrance through which she came.*)

BELINDA. Oh, Lady Sibyl! 'Ow 'ideous! 'Ow unbearable!

(*Enter* **LADY SIBYL PONSONBY,** *twenty-four. Both are charmingly dressed as of the eighteenth century in some textile-like tapa cloth.* **LADY SIBYL** *is a great lady, however, and carries a parasol tufted with seagulls' feathers.*)

LADY SIBYL. *(staring at* **GULLIVER,** *but with more controlled repulsion; as though to herself.)* It's hall true! Then it's hall true, wot they say! *(pronounced "si")*

BELINDA. *(to* **GULLIVER,** *spitefully)* Turn your fice awigh! How can you look at Lady Sibyl?

LADY SIBYL. *(with authority)* 'Old your tongue, Jenkins.

BELINDA. *(pointing)* But he's terrible! He's terrible!

LADY SIBYL. *(coldly)* Yes. – You are 'ideous to behold.

GULLIVER. I'm a plain man, madam; and in addition I have been without food and drink for three days – and with very little sleep.

LADY SIBYL. *(again as though to herself)* I have never seen an old man before. *Forty*-six, you say? It's hall true, too true.

BELINDA. *(peeking from behind* **LADY SIBYL***)* The wrinkles, your ladyship. Nobody could count them! – Can he see? Can he hear?

LADY SIBYL. *(from curiosity, not kindness)* You must be suffering in every part of your body?

GULLIVER. I have suffered, madam, principally from thirst until I found this spring here; and I would be most beholden to you if *you* could also graciously give me something to eat.

LADY SIBYL. I shall never forget this moment. You are, indeed, a most pitiable spectacle.

GULLIVER. *(with dignity)* I shall turn my face away if it distresses you, madam.

BELINDA. All of you is as repulsive as your face.

GULLIVER. I am as God made me and the hardships I have endured. – If you would graciously provide me with the means I could catch fish to [assuage] my hunger. I have been shipwrecked before and have sustained myself in many ways.

LADY SIBYL. *(musing)* At your age everything must be painful – exceedingly – breathing…and walking…

GULLIVER. *(loud)* Young woman, are you indeed deaf *(pronounced "deef")* or do you lack humanity? I am starving.

BELINDA. "Young woman!" You are talking to Lady Sibyl Ponsonby.

LADY SIBYL. Be quiet, Jenkins. – Old man, you will be given something to eat. There have been other old men on this island. They were given something to eat before they departed.

GULLIVER. I hope that will not be long.

LADY SIBYL. That will not be long.

GULLIVER. Did I understand you, madam, did I hear correctly: that you have never seen a man of forty-six before?

BELINDA. Forty-six! No one has ever seen anyone older than twenty-nine – except one that floated up from the sea, like yourself. There is no one on this island older than twenty-nine and there never will be.

GULLIVER. Merciful Heavens! What do you do with your older persons?

LADY SIBYL. I will now go and call someone to attend to your needs. You will not follow me! You will not leave this place. Today is a day of festival and it is of the highest importance that no one sees you – that is, as few as possible see you. – Jenkins, stay near him.

BELINDA. I, your ladyship!!

LADY SIBYL. Do not enter into conversation with him. *(appraising him coldly)* I do not think he could progress far.

BELINDA. *(becoming hysterical)* Oh, your ladyship, your ladyship – do not leave me alone with him. I will become ill with the sight. *(She falls on her knees, clinging to* **LADY SIBYL.***)* I will become ill. I will become ill.

LADY SIBYL. Get up, Jenkins! – Very well, I will stay with this man. Go to the Duke of Cornwall. Draw him aside and speak to him in a low voice. Tell him that we have come upon this…foreigner. 'E will know what to do.

GULLIVER. *(gesturing as though bringing food to his mouth)* And tell him –

LADY SIBYL. Tell him the old man is hungry. – But, Jenkins, hold your tongue. Do not speak of it to anyone else.

BELINDA. To think that this should happen today – of all days! *(She sidles up toward* **GULLIVER** *and examines him intently. Softly.)* Think of all the years he has lived!

LADY SIBYL. Jenkins!

BELINDA. *(Still scanning* **GULLIVER**; *half answering.)* Yes, milady.

LADY SIBYL. Jenkins! Do as I tell you!

BELINDA. Yes, milady; but I shall never see an old man again. I want to look at him… *(lower)* …he is not as abominable as he was at first. One gets used to him, a little. – Old man, have you wives…and children?

LADY SIBYL. Belinda! I shall have you jailed!

BELINDA. *(turning to her, with spirit)* Your ladyship, with all due respect to your ladyship, your ladyship has been extremely severe with me for many weeks. I care not if I go to jail. As I was the first person to see this old man I ask to be permitted to have a few words with him.

LADY SIBYL. Two minutes, Belinda…No more.

*(***LADY SIBYL*** turns her back on them and moves to the rear of the scene, striking her parasol on the floor.)*

GULLIVER. Yes, Mistress Jenkins, I have a wife Mary, a son John, and a daughter Betsy.

BELINDA. *(slowly, scarcely a question)* And are you very cruel to them?

GULLIVER. Madam?

BELINDA. *Old* men are cruel and nasty tempered. Everyone knows that.

(GULLIVER gazes deep into her eyes with a faint smile, slowly shaking his head. She continues, as if to herself.)

Your eyes are different from our eyes. Maybe some old men are a *little bit* kind.

(GULLIVER, as though in friendly complicity, rubs his stomach with one hand and conveys the other to his mouth.)

Yes, I will hurry. – I am going, your ladyship.

LADY SIBYL. And remember, no blabbing. *(She looks toward the sun, almost directly overhead.)* The games are about to begin. When you have delivered your message, take your place in silence.

BELINDA. *(curtsies)* Yes, your ladyship.

(BELINDA goes out. LADY SIBYL starts strolling about with great self-possession.)

GULLIVER. Surely, I did not hear correctly – *no* older men?

LADY SIBYL. I have no wish to enter into conversation with you.

GULLIVER. *(After a short pause, no longer able to contain himself.)* By God's body, madam, you cannot be of stone! You are not a child! I have not hitherto been regarded as a contemptible being. I have been received by kings and queens and have been their guest at meat…I am Captain Lemuel Gulliver. I am not a dog.

LADY SIBYL. I have never seen a dog, but I think you must greatly resemble one.

GULLIVER. Madam, you have seen nothing but one small island. You are not in a position to say that you have seen anything. I am astonished that you have no questions to put to me about the world that surrounds you.

LADY SIBYL. *(lofty smile)* What questions would those be, Captain Gullibo?

GULLIVER. Madam, ignorance is a misery, but there is one still greater: a lack of any desire to increase one's knowledge.

LADY SIBYL. But I have learned much from you in this short time. You have come from that world out there *(She indicates it lightly with her parasol; her voice turns suddenly vindictive.)* and you have brought its poisons with you. Your visible infirmities are also marks of the country from which you came. They must be as painful for you to bear as for us to behold. However, you will not have to bear them much longer.

(GULLIVER gives up trying to understand her. He sinks down on the bench by the table. He is about to fall asleep.)

Captain, it is not our custom for a commoner to be seated in the presence of the nobility.

(GULLIVER, uncomprehending, raises his head.)

I see; you are deaf. *(pronounced "deef")* I said: it is not the custom for a commoner to be seated in the presence of the nobility.

GULLIVER. *(dragging himself to his feet; with ironic deference)* Oh...oh...your ladyship will forgive me...my fatigue... and my hunger.

(LADY SIBYL puts her hand into her reticule and brings out some lozenges, which she places on the table.)

LADY SIBYL. While you are waiting, here are some comfits which I have been keeping...for my children.

GULLIVER. For your children, Lady Sibyl?

LADY SIBYL. Our children on this island live in a village of their own. They are well tended. They are happy. That is our custom here.

(In astonishment, GULLIVER is about to ask a question. He corrects himself, and, bowing, says in a low voice.)

GULLIVER. I thank your ladyship.

> *(He puts two into his mouth ravenously; then takes one out for decorum's sake. A musical sound, like a rolling chord from many harps, is heard from the city.* **GULLIVER** *listens in astonishment.)*

May I ask your ladyship the source of that music?

LADY SIBYL. You forget everything you are told. Today is a day of great festival. *(She looks at the sun.)* It is beginning with the children's Morris Dance and –

GULLIVER. Oh, milady, I would greatly wish to see this festival –

LADY SIBYL. *(slight laugh, "how unthinkable")* These will be followed by the Hoop Dance and the Dagger Dance. The Duke of Cornwall – who will be here in a moment – is the greatest victor in the Hoop Dance that has ever been known. He has won eight garlands. Moreover, he is the only man who has ever kept a kite in the air for an entire day.

GULLIVER. Ah!! He must indeed be remarkable!…An entire day!…I trust that the duke is of mature years?

LADY SIBYL. *(sharply)* I did not hear you correctly. (**GULLIVER** *does not repeat the question.)* He is naturally of mature years. He is our governor. He is twenty-eight *(pronounced "'ite").*

GULLIVER. *(stares at her; then with dawning horror)* Great Heavens, girl! What do you do with your older persons?

LADY SIBYL. Captain Gullibo, there is no profit in pursuing a conversation on matters you are not capable of understanding.

GULLIVER. *(shouting)* You kill them. You murder them when they reach the age of twenty-nine?

LADY SIBYL. How dare you address me in that manner? – Vulgar brutish Englander! Barbarian! How could you understand customs that are based on wisdom and reason.

GULLIVER. I dread to hear them! *(louder)* Are you able to answer me: what do you do to those who reach the age of twenty-nine?

LADY SIBYL. *(slowly; with serene assurance)* We drink the wine. We sleep. We are placed in a boat. The current carries us away.

GULLIVER. Thunder! This is hellish!

LADY SIBYL. *(putting a hand delicately on her ear)* Restrine your senile violence, Captain Gullibo.

GULLIVER. And *you*, your ladyship – are you going to drink that wine and go to sleep in that boat?

LADY SIBYL. When I am old – readily, gladly. I have four years to live. That is a very long time.

GULLIVER. And no one ever rebels? No one twenty-nine years old ever wishes to live longer?

LADY SIBYL. Captain Gullibo, you prate. You rive. You forget that you are old – very old. What I have told you is the custom of this island! Do you understand the word "custom"?…Would any of us *wish* to be…

GULLIVER. *(hand to head)* Your ladyship must permit me to sit down. *(he does)*

LADY SIBYL. *(strolling about and fanning herself)* It is understandable that the duke is occupied today. *(severely)* Your arrival is most inopportune.

GULLIVER. The matter was beyond my control, Lady Sibyl. Little did I know that I was arriving on this happy island on the great day of the Hoop Dance. On future occasions I shall arrange it with greater propriety.

LADY SIBYL. *(looks at him and raises her eyebrows)* Future occasions, Captain Gullibo? At your age, Captain, you cannot speak with certainty of future occasions.

GULLIVER. *(returning her glance; in a low voice)* Lady Sibyl, I am thinking of your children. You will never know the joys of seeing them grow into young manhood and womanhood. You will never hold grandchildren on your knees.

LADY SIBYL. You are tedious, Captain Gullibo. I have read of those things in books.

GULLIVER. Ah, madam. – You have books, I see.

LADY SIBYL. We have one hundred and twenty-seven books, Captain.

GULLIVER. *(lowers his head in admiration; after a pause, suddenly humble and earnest)* Lady Sibyl, let me throw myself upon your mercy. You are a woman, and women in all times have tempered this rough world with mercy and compassion. I have arrived a stranger and an interloper here; I do not wish to intrude upon this happy existence. I can see that you have much influence on this island; graciously exert it on my behalf. I saw that there were boats drawn up along the shore. I am a seaman of experience. When I have been given some food to stay my hunger, be my advocate with this Duke of Cornwall –

LADY SIBYL. *(purest amazement)* Where would you go?

GULLIVER. *(pointing)* …That island or continent…those mountains…

LADY SIBYL. *(harshly)* I have nothing to do with such matters. Those fishing boats and their sails are fixed to the shore. They are locked with thongs that only a few nobles can undo. – You forget that you are old – very old. Your life is over. Anyone can see that.

(She turns away.)

GULLIVER. I have a wife and children. – You said you have children?

LADY SIBYL. Naturally I have children.

GULLIVER. Look in your heart. Enable me to –

LADY SIBYL. Be silent!

GULLIVER. *(sinking onto the bench; to himself, in despair)* Yes… yes…Humanity is the last thing that will be learned by man. *(He puts his head on his arms and is about to fall asleep.)*

LADY SIBYL. *(walking up and down, loftily)* You may be certain that nothing will be done here that is not for the wisest and the best. We are enlightened here; and we are Christians. That strain of music you heard came from Westminster Abbey. The Archbishop of Canterbury is addressing the contestants in the games. If you were a *young* man we would be proud to show you how happy our existence is, and how perfect our institutions. This perfection is rendered possible by the fact that here we have no –

(**GULLIVER** *has fallen asleep.*)

GULLIVER. *(mumbling)* …steep…the steep streets… Redriff, home!…Mary – Polly!…Polly, forgive me….

(*He falls silent.* **LADY SIBYL** *gazes at him for a moment with repugnance, then draws nearer and scans his face intently – a long gaze. When he stirs and seems about to wake, she moves away and, opening her parasol, strolls off the stage.*)

(*In deep stupor* **GULLIVER** *slips off the bench and rolls under the table.*)

(**LADY SIBYL** *returns hurriedly; there is a suggestion of walking backward as though royalty were approaching. Enter the* **DUKE OF CORNWALL,** *twenty-eight, very splendid in festival dress. To the early eighteenth-century costume have been added feathers and colored shells, etc. He is followed by* **SIMPSON,** *twenty, a commoner, carrying a tray of food. The* **DUKE** *gazes fixedly at* **GULLIVER.***)

LADY SIBYL. He has fallen into a swound, your grace.

DUKE. Simpson – throw some water on his face.

(**SIMPSON** *scoops some water from the mirror pool and throws it on* **GULLIVER***'s face.* **GULLIVER** *recovers consciousness, stirs and cumbrously extricates himself from under the table. Finally, he grasps the situation and, standing erect, confronts the* **DUKE,** *eye to eye.*)

Who are you?

GULLIVER. Lemuel Gulliver, your grace, captain of the fourmaster *Arcturus,* Port of London.

DUKE. How old are you?

GULLIVER. I am in my middle years; I am forty-six.

DUKE. They tell me you have been three days without food – Simpson, place the food on the table. Eat!

GULLIVER. I thank your grace. Commoners do not sit in the presence of the nobility. I shall eat when you have left to take part in the festival. *(pause)* Sir, I have visited many countries and have been shipwrecked on the shores of several. In all of them, save one, I have been treated with courtesy as a citizen of England and a subject of our gracious sovereign, Queen Anne. I am indebted to you for this relief from my hunger. I trust that hereafter I may see your cities and learn of your customs. In return I shall gladly tell you of other parts of the world that I have visited; and above all of the country whose language you speak and from which your ancestors came.

DUKE. *(again a short contemptuous pause; then with a curt gesture of the hand)* You are tedious, old man. – Simpson!

SIMPSON. Yes, your grace?

DUKE. Withdraw to a distance. It is not suitable that a commoner hear this nonsense. I shall call you when it is time for you to stand watch over the captain.

(**SIMPSON** *bows and goes out.* **GULLIVER** *begins to laugh to himself and, turning away, sits down.)*

LADY SIBYL. *(revolted)* He is laughing!!

GULLIVER. To be young, and yet ask no questions about the country from which your ancestors came! To be young, and yet have no curiosity concerning the shore that lies upon the horizon! To be young, and yet – oh, ye immortal Gods! – to be without adventure of mind or generosity of spirit! Now it is clear to me why you so gladly bring your lives to a close at the age of twenty-nine – *gladly* was Lady Sibyl's word.

DUKE. *(bitingly)* That should not be difficult for you to understand – you, with this decay of mind and body –

GULLIVER. *(interrupting)* No! No, it is not the advance of age that frightens you on this island. *(with a sardonic smile)* A greater enemy threatens you. *(abruptly changing the subject)* I do not wish to detain your grace from the festival and from your trophies.

DUKE. Come, Lady Sibyl.

GULLIVER. Permit me, however, one question.

(*The* **DUKE** *nods.*)

What is the name of this island and this country?

DUKE. Name? Why should it have a name?

GULLIVER. I have visited twenty countries. Each has borne a name in which it takes pride.

DUKE. Proud? All of them were proud?

GULLIVER. They were. They are.

DUKE. Among those twenty countries was there one that was not governed by old men – governed, misgoverned, burdened, oppressed by old men? By the pride and avarice, and the lust for power of old men? One which did not constantly war at the instigation of old men like *yourself,* to enlarge its boundaries; to enslave others; to enrich itself? We know of the War of the Roses. Or by the religious bigotry of old men – we know of the Saint Bartholomew Massacre, [the] murder of Charles, king and martyr. And when these prides of yours have obtained their lands, whose bodies are those lying upon the field of battle? – They are the bodies of men under thirty. We need no name to distinguish this country from others. Say that you are in the Country of the Young.

GULLIVER. So be it! – Since you do not wish me to encumber you longer, I request some boat with which I may rid you of my presence. (*in amazement*) How did you come here? Who brought you here?

DUKE. God!

GULLIVER. God! – Where did you acquire this distrust and hatred of the old?

DUKE. We have no boats for that purpose.

GULLIVER. The smallest would serve me.

DUKE. No boat of ours has ever made that journey and never will.

GULLIVER. Perhaps your grace will let me purchase a boat. This ring was given to me by the King of Laputa. It is of pure alchemist's gold.

DUKE. You have been here a few hours. Lady Sibyl has told me that already you have offered us insult and have spoken of our customs with contempt; and now you wish to introduce barter and trafficking, and gold! – gold, which is above all the instrument by which old men keep the younger in subjection. There is no gold and no trading here. You shall never leave this island and you shall not long envenom it. We shall make you a present for which we ask no return. We shall give you the only happiness that still lies open to you.

GULLIVER. Duke of Cornwall – Duke of Palm Trees and Sand! I wish you a happy twenty-ninth birthday. I can understand that you will gladly drink the wine and welcome the long sleep. Twenty-nine years of jumping through hoops and flying kites will have been enough. Already you are advancing toward a decay worse than age – yes, toward boredom, infinite boredom. Youth left to itself is a cork upon the waves. As we say of the young: they do not know what to do with themselves. It is only under the severity – the well-wishing severity – of your elders that you can shake from yourselves the misery of your aimless state. You elect yourselves into societies and call yourselves dukes and earls; did I hear correctly that each man on this island has several wives? You play games. What more can you ask of a thirtieth birthday than a deep slumber!

LADY SIBYL. *(ablate)* Your grace! How can you let him speak to you so?!

DUKE. *(with a smile)* But this is what we knew; foul and embittered age! Envy and jealousy! Despising those things of which he is no longer capable. *(whimsically to* **LADY SIBYL***)* Perhaps we should take this man and exhibit him for all to see.

LADY SIBYL. *(covering her face)* Your grace!

GULLIVER. Yes, and for all to hear, your grace.

DUKE. And to hear. – What would you say to them?

GULLIVER. Why, I should tell them that if a man is not civilized between the ages of twelve and twenty – civilized by his elders – he will never be civilized at all. (**LADY SIBYL** *covers her ears.*) And oh, it is not an easy task. To educate young men is like rolling boulders up to the tops of mountains; the whole community is engaged in the work and with what doubtful success! For every *one* Isaac Newton or Christopher Wren there are thousands who roll to the bottom of the mountain and occupy themselves with jumping through hoops. *(He sways from weakness, his hand to his head and heart.)* Go to your dances and garlands. I can see that your happiness has begun to stale already. You are weary of life. Old age has marked you already.

DUKE. *(with supreme complaisance)* Oh, I'm young enough! *(he calls)* Mr. Simpson! Mr. Simpson!!

(The sound of music has been rising from the distance. Enter **SIMPSON.***)*

SIMPSON. Yes, your grace?

DUKE. Simpson, you are in charge of this man. See that he does not leave this clearing. Do not enter into conversation with him. It would suffocate you. Later I shall send someone to replace you – Lady Sibyl!

*(***LADY SIBYL***'s hand has gone to her forehead; her parasol and reticule fall. She is about to faint.)*

LADY SIBYL. Oh, your grace…this sight…has sickened me.

DUKE. *(cold fury)* Take command of yourself!

(With a gesture he orders **SIMPSON** *to pick up the fallen objects.* **SIMPSON** *does so and holds them ready for* **LADY SIBYL.***)*

LADY SIBYL. *(swaying; with closed eyes)* I must breathe a moment.

DUKE. Fool! *(He strikes her sharply on both cheeks.)* Go to the city!

GULLIVER. *(taking two steps forward)* You strike her!! You strike her!

DUKE. We permit no weakness here – neither ours nor yours.

GULLIVER. *(turns and seats himself on the bench by the table)* Humanity is the last thing that will be learned by man; it will not be learned from the young.

*(**LADY SIBYL** has taken her parasol and reticule. She collects her dignity, but is scarcely able to leave the stage.)*

DUKE. Simpson!

SIMPSON. Your grice!

DUKE. If you fail at any point in your guard over this man, you will be put to the press – and you know what press I mean. And you will be removed from your office as builder and constructor. *(He looks appraisingly at **GULLIVER**.)* If he tries to leave the clearing, kick him strongly at the shinbones.

*(He goes out. **SIMPSON** takes his stand at a distance from **GULLIVER** whom he watches intently. **GULLIVER** returns to his meal, but seems to have lost his appetite. Again there is a sound of music from the city. **GULLIVER** rises and listens.)*

GULLIVER. Is there no way, Mr. Simpson, that I may view the games from a distance?
*(**SIMPSON** shakes his head.)*
I am sorry. *(He eats a little.)* They must be a wonderful sight…wonderful. Hoops and kites. *(pause)* You strike women…is that often, Mr. Simpson?…Do you strike women frequently, Mr. Simpson? *(no reply)* …You are very proud of your civilization…when you are angry you *strike* and you *torture*… *(**SIMPSON** mutters something.)* I did not hear what you said, Mr. Simpson.

SIMPSON. He is old. Strikes and tortures because 'e is old. 'E will die next year.

GULLIVER. He will be killed next year. That is not quite the same thing as merely dying. He will be killed. No wonder he is excitable, Mr. Simpson. In the normal way of life we grow of a more mild and kindly disposition with the years. *(He eats.)* So you are a builder and constructor, Mr. Simpson. You are an architect. Lady Sibyl spoke of a Westminster Abbey. I would like to see it. Did you build this Westminster Abbey, sir? *(no answer)* You have great storms in this part of the world – far greater than London has. You must build very – solidly. Have you rock here?

(SIMPSON points off. GULLIVER rises and peers in the direction.)

Coral limestone, I presume. Not easy. Arches and a vaulted roof. Ah, you should see the dome of St. Paul's. There's a sight, Mr. Simpson… *(he eats)* I am glad that you feel no disposition to talk, sir. I was afraid that you might ask me questions about the life led by young men like yourself in my country. *(pause)* It would fill me with shame to describe it to you. *(He lowers his voice as though imparting a discreditable secret.)* Imagine it! You would be working all the time to acquire more knowledge: from morning to night – and at night by lamplight. Think: to be a better doctor, to govern the people more wisely, *to be a better builder*, Mr. Simpson. Go down on your knees, sir, and thank your Maker that you live on this happy island where learning never penetrates, where young men are not encouraged by old men to extend their knowledge and their skill.

SIMPSON. *(loudly)* The old men drive them like slaves; the old men take the credit and the profit.

GULLIVER. The young men succeed them. They are not killed at twenty-nine. They become master builders themselves and may decide whether they will be just or unjust. However, I do not wish to talk about it. I reproach myself that I am preventing you from taking part in the games.

SIMPSON. Commoners do not take part in the games.

GULLIVER. Ah! *(he eats)*

(SIMPSON gazes at him, brooding)

SIMPSON. I'm a builder.

GULLIVER. *(looking up at the summerhouse)* Ah! – you made this?

SIMPSON. Aye – and the new Westminster Abbey.

GULLIVER. Westminster Abbey! Then you are the chief builder.

SIMPSON. The chief builder is an earl. He has no time to build.

GULLIVER. The new Abbey is of stone – of sandstone or coral?

SIMPSON. The pillars at the corners are.

GULLIVER. And the roof?

(**SIMPSON** *shakes his head.* **GULLIVER** *points to the thatch.*)

Of thatch? – of palm boughs?

(**SIMPSON** *nods.*)

But, man, you have severe storms here. Ah! *(he looks up)* Mr. Simpson, the storm that cast me on your shores has damaged this charming…shelter, this pagoda. Was your Westminster Abbey able to sustain the fury of that wind and rain?

(**SIMPSON** *stares straight before him.*)

You will not answer me, man! Your Abbey seats – what? – four hundred. Of what is your roof? Of palm fronds?

(**SIMPSON**, *without moving his eyes, nods.*)

I see! When storm destroys your Westminster Abbey you build another. I see! I see! You don't know how to make an arch or a buttress. Oh, Mr. Simpson, do not ask me the secrets of the arch, the buttress and the dome. You are happy. Remain happy. Do not let us think of all the labor that went into those discoveries.

SIMPSON. *(taking steps toward* **GULLIVER**; *in a low voice)* Sir… Mr. Captain… *(His hands describe an arch.)* Do you know how to pile stone…so they will not fall?

GULLIVER. Believe me. Mr. Simpson, I did not arrive in this paradise in order to poison it with thoughts of progress and industry.

SIMPSON. But you *do* know?

GULLIVER. Perhaps in a hundred years some unhappy youth will be born with talent – with genius. *He* will light upon the laws of the arch. He will prove that youth stands in no need of its elders, no need of the accumulated wisdom of its ancestors. *He will make a roof*…Bring your ear nearer, young man the dome of St. Paul's… *(His hand descries a high dome.)*

SIMPSON. How high is it?

GULLIVER. How high? Sixty men standing on one another's shoulders could not touch the top of it.

SIMPSON. *(back three yards)* You are lying! All old men lie. Eat your food. Go to sleep. I ask you a question and you give me a lie.

(**SIMPSON** *has raised his head.*)

GULLIVER. What I said is true, but your rebuke is justified. There is no greater unkindness than to arouse ambition in a young man. – But *you* are to blame. You asked me a question. *(with assumed indignation)* A few more questions like that and you'll be proposing that we take a *boat* and cross to that shore. No I'll not go, I tell you.

SIMPSON. *(sullenly)* The boats are tied and we cannot untie them.

GULLIVER. Yes, those thongs the nobles keep… *(His eyes are looking off speculatively.)*

SIMPSON. They're twisted and untwisted with hooks of iron.

GULLIVER. Iron?

SIMPSON. Aye, they're the only pieces of metal on the island. The nobles keep them.

GULLIVER. Very wise! Some fool might think of journeying out there…for knowledge and science. – Understand, young man, I'll not leave this island. Give me this day here; then bring the wine and the long sleep. Why should a man trouble his head raising domes? Fly kites, jump through hoops, beget children and sleep.

SIMPSON. *(after a pause, grumbling unintelligibly)* These things you call secrets…

GULLIVER. I cannot understand you, sir.

SIMPSON. These things you call the secrets of the arch and the…batless – old men keep these secrets to themselves, that's certain.

GULLIVER. *(sternly)* Cease, Mr. Simpson, to talk of things you know nothing about.

SIMPSON. How would a young man learn them?

GULLIVER. You are asking dangerous questions, Mr. Simpson. – Let me bid you again to go down on your knees and thank your Maker that you do not live in a country where older men would urge you and struggle with you and encourage you to enrich yourself with all learning and skill.

SIMPSON. I don't believe you.

GULLIVER. – A young man would learn them by crossing that water and finding his way into a world that does not spend all its time in games and dances.

SIMPSON. *(mumbles)* I do not believe you. *(suddenly loud)* All old men are wicked.

GULLIVER. *(simply)* I am the only old man you have ever seen.

SIMPSON. *(approaching* **GULLIVER,** *the beginning of violence)* Then tell me –

GULLIVER. What?

SIMPSON. The secrets: the arch and the batless.

GULLIVER. *(backing away)* I do not know them.

SIMPSON. *(seizing* **GULLIVER***'s throat)* Tell me them! Wicked old man, tell me them!

GULLIVER. *(forced to his knees)* I am not a builder. I am a doctor and a seaman.

SIMPSON. *(as they struggle)* I will not let you go before you tell me –

(**GULLIVER** *faints. Pause.* **SIMPSON** *leans over him and calls:)*

Old man! Old man!

(Enter **BELINDA** *carrying a tray and more fruit. She starts back in consternation.)*

BELINDA. *(whispering)* Is he dead?…Have *you* killed him?

SIMPSON. *(sullenly)* No…he has died of his old age.

*(***BELINDA** *puts her ear to* **GULLIVER**'s *mouth.)*

BELINDA. I think he is still breathing. It is a swound. *(Both are on their knees gazing at* **GULLIVER**.*)* Now I do not think he is ugly at all. I think he is a friend.

SIMPSON. *(moves away in inner turmoil)* I do not understand a word he says. He should not have come here.

BELINDA. *(as before)* What a strange thing wrinkles are. *(Unconsciously she strokes her face…softly.)* I could ask him questions all day. – Mr. Simpson, let him go back to his own people.

SIMPSON. *(harshly)* How could he do that?

*(***BELINDA** *slowly draws from her apron pocket a hook of iron.* **SIMPSON** *draws back in horror.)*

BELINDA. *(lowering her voice)* This is the hook that was lost last year. It was on Lady Sibyl's dressing table. I think she put it there for me to find it. I think she has hidden it to spite the Duke of Cornwall. *(She holds it out toward* **SIMPSON**.*)* Unlock the boat and let the man go.

SIMPSON. No!

BELINDA. *(Gazes at* **GULLIVER**. *Pause. Low, with energy.)* Go with him!…He is not strong enough to sail the boat alone. Go.

SIMPSON. Do not speak to me! No, I will not go…among other men…I do not know anything. *He* does not know that we commoners cannot read. Every – *over there* – would see that I am a booby.

BELINDA. Mr. Simpson! Look at him. Come close and look at him! He would be your friend…I think *some* old people are good.

SIMPSON. No, I will not go.

BELINDA. He is waking up. Go away and think; but take the hook.

(**SIMPSON** *takes the hook and goes off.*)

GULLIVER. *(Opens his eyes. Pause. Sees **BELINDA**.)* Oh! You are here…Where is the young man?

BELINDA. He is nearby…will you tell me your name again?

GULLIVER. Captain Gulliver.

BELINDA. Captain Gulliver. If you came to your home again what would you do first?

GULLIVER. Mistress Jenkins, I would go up the steep street – you have never seen a steep street! – I think it would be at sunset…I would knock at the door…My wife or one of my children would come to the door… *(pause)* …Soon we would sit down at the table, and give thanks to God…and eat…

BELINDA. *(laughing, scandalized)* Captain Gulliver, you would sit down with your wife!!

GULLIVER. Do not husband and wives –

BELINDA. No – !! *(She laughs.)* Sit down! No man has ever eaten with a woman – ! The men eat all by themselves. The nobles in one place. The commoners in another. And the boys when they are six by themselves.

GULLIVER. And if I lived on this happy island, when would I see my daughter? *(She does not answer.)* You remember your father?

BELINDA. Yes.

GULLIVER. You saw him often? You loved him?

BELINDA. But…men live…*over there…*

GULLIVER. The childhood of the race…You have slipped five-ten thousand years…

(**SIMPSON** *has returned, and half hidden, is listening.*)

In a thousand years, Mistress Jenkins, gradually on this island things will change. A man will have one wife and only one wife. I think when your father died at twenty-nine he was just beginning to understand (**GULLIVER** *points to his forehead.*) what the joys of being your father could be – but it was too late.

(**GULLIVER** *clasps* **BELINDA** *by her shoulders, sadly*)

GULLIVER. *(cont.)* You all die here just before a new world of mind and heart is open to you.

(The music and sounds of celebration have increased, as if approaching. **SIMPSON** *breaks from his hiding place and rushes to* **GULLIVER** *with the iron hook.* **SIMPSON** *pulls at* **GULLIVER***'s arm and points toward the sea.* **GULLIVER** *grasps the situation immediately, starts to go with* **SIMPSON***, but looks back at* **BELINDA***. She remains motionless, staring straight ahead, and does not meet his glance.* **SIMPSON** *drags* **GULLIVER** *off.)*

(Music is louder. **BELINDA** *gazes front; intense, conflicted. Pause.)*

*(***SIMPSON** *reappears running. He takes both of* **BELINDA***'s hands in his. They look at each other. A decision passes between them.* **BELINDA** *casts one glance back over her shoulder at all she has ever known; and they run off to join* **GULLIVER***.)*

(Music increases.)

(Two **BOY GUARDS***, fifteen, rush in with ropes to bind* **GULLIVER** *for his ceremonial death. The* **DUKE** *enters behind. They look about, see that* **GULLIVER***,* **SIMPSON** *and* **BELINDA** *are gone. The* **DUKE** *is the first to realize the implication of this absence. He stands upstage center as the* **GUARDS** *roughly search everywhere. Convinced that the man they were after has escaped, they turn to the* **DUKE***.)*

(Music takes on a wild, threatening sound.)

(The **DUKE** *has been gazing out toward a horizon, perhaps seeing the boat moving off, perhaps contemplating his own soon wasted mortality. The* **BOY GUARDS** *gaze intently at him as the lights fade)*

End of Play

A NOTE ON THE TEXT

The author's manuscript existed in a partial typescript, which contained Wilder's handwritten corrections interleaved with several handwritten pages of clearly indicated revised material. The author's manuscript ended with Gulliver's speech to Belinda, spoken while Simpson listens hidden from their view. To conclude the play for production, I felt it would be helpful to take into account Wilder's most plausible intention: that Swift's Gulliver, only borrowed for this adventure, be returned safely to London and his place in English literature.

What then of Simpson and Belinda? Belinda had earlier insisted to Simpson that Gulliver was not strong enough to make the trip alone. Her plea that Simpson accompany Gulliver in the escape strongly suggests that Wilder intended Simpson and Gulliver to leave the island together. Simpson had been sent off with the tool that unlocks the boats. Further, there is the duke's threat that Simpson will be put to the press if he fails in his guard duties. Will Belinda stay behind to face the wrath of the Duke? Gulliver has developed a strong paternal feeling for her and, in addition, she and Simpson are commoners, both of age, both bright and interested and curious by nature: a matched set to be saved on Gulliver's "ark."

And the Duke? Wilder often placed characters in a position where, experiencing an epiphany, they catch a glimpse of what lies ahead. *Youth* seems constructed for just such a moment. The twenty-eight-year-old duke, himself within a year of his enforced demise, returns as he must, accompanied by his callow bullyish guards. Might Wilder perhaps have wanted us to wonder what the Duke feels about the defeat of his will and authority in the light of what he will not be able to avoid in a year's time? Those questions hang in the added final tableau.

F. J. O'Neil
April 1997

THORNTON WILDER (1897-1975) was an accomplished novelist and playwright whose works explore the connection between the commonplace and the cosmic dimensions of human experience. He won three Pulitzer Prizes: for his novel *The Bridge of San Luis Rey*, and two plays, *Our Town* and *The Skin of Our Teeth*. Wilder's farce, *The Matchmaker*, was adapted as the musical *Hello, Dolly!* He also enjoyed enormous success as a translator, adaptor, actor, librettist and lecturer/teacher. Wilder's many honors include the Gold Medal for Fiction from the American Academy of Arts and Letters and the Presidential Medal of Freedom. Penelope Niven's definitive biography, *Thornton Wilder: A Life*, was published in October 2012. For more information, please visit www.thorntonwilder.com.

Also by
Thornton Wilder

The Beaux' Stratagem (with Ken Ludwig)
The Matchmaker
The Alcestiad
Our Town
The Skin of Our Teeth

Thornton Wilder One Act Series: The Ages of Man
Infancy
Childhood
Youth
The Rivers Under the Earth

Thornton Wilder One Act Series: The Seven Deadly Sins
The Drunken Sisters
Bernice
The Wreck on the 5:25
A Ringing of Doorbells
In Shakespeare and the Bible
Someone From Assisi
Cement Hands

Thornton Wilder One Act Series: Wilder's Classic One Acts
The Long Christmas Dinner
Queens of France
Pullman Car Hiawatha
Love and How to Cure It
Such Things Only Happen in Books
The Happy Journey to Trenton and Camden

www.thorntonwilder.com

www.ingramcontent.com/pod-product-compliance
Lightning Source LLC
Chambersburg PA
CBHW070422120726
47909CB00005B/1762